This book belongs to:

_____

My pet's names are:

_____

My favorite animals are:

_____

# Mimi and Maty to the Rescue!

Book 1

Roger the Rat is on the loose!

Written by Brooke Smith
Illustrated by Alli Arnold

Better World Kids Books
New York

Sky Pony Press
New York

To Kelly and Mimi:
    Two big hearts that make mine whole.
And for Dad... forever and always.

                    — Brooke

For Harry and Nino, my fuzzy boys.

                    — Alli

Sky Pony Press books may be purchased in bulk at special discounts for sales promotion, corporate gifts, fund-raising, or educational purposes. Special editions can also be created to specifications. For details, contact the Special Sales Department, Sky Pony Press, 307 West 36th Street, 11th Floor, New York, NY 10018 or info@skyhorsepublishing.com.

Sky Pony® is a registered trademark of Skyhorse Publishing, Inc.®, a Delaware corporation.

Visit our website at www.skyponypress.com.

10 9 8 7 6 5 4 3 2 1

Manufactured in China, May 2012
This product conforms to CPSIA 2008

Library of Congress Cataloging-in-Publication Data is available on file.

ISBN: 978-1-62087-252-9

CHAPTER ONE

I got a super
special notebook in the mail today.

It came in a bright yellow envelope.

My Aunt Bee sent it to me. She's a beekeeper. (Yep, Bee's a beekeeper.) You know . . . those people who wear huge hoods and gloves and get to play with bees all day.

She also sent a new bandana for my dog, Maty.

I rescued Maty from the animal shelter. She has big brown eyes and a sweet, sweet smile.

Oh, and three legs.

Maty got a super bad infection in her leg when she was just a pup, so she had to have an operation to remove the leg. But lucky for Maty, the animal shelter took her in and took really good care of her, and that's where I found my very best friend in the whole wide world!

And Maty doesn't mind that she only has three legs—
she's up for anything! Bike rides, beach time, birthday
parties . . . and Maty can catch a frisbee better than
any dog I've ever met!

Anyway, rescuing Maty was so much fun that I decided
I wanted to help tons more animals.

Last year when I was visiting Aunt Bee's farm, I rescued a little bird with a broken wing.

I even saved a butterfly from drowning in a rain puddle!

Oh yeah, and a baby chipmunk that
wandered away from her mom.

That's why Aunt Bee sent me a notebook, so I can keep track of all of my animal rescues this summer. I'm not sure there'll be a lot of rescue action around here, but it's a cool idea. It'd be great to spend some of my summer break helping animals.

Hmmm . . . maybe I'll ask some of my friends if they know any animals that need help.

Maybe one of their pets or their neighbors' pets or their dentists' pets has gone missing or is in trouble or something.

I better start writing this stuff down in my new notebook.

Friday:

Call my friends —
 Ruby, Skip, Henry,
Arnie (allergic to furry
animals, but has a chameleon)
Dylan, Sadie, George
+ the Tiny Twins!!!
    ↖ they have ② of
            everything.

✳ TELL EVERYBODY
that Maty and I are now
official ANIMAL RESCUERS!
That means we are
going to help animals
BIG TIME.

And Maty and I should probably put up some posters around town . . . to get the word out.

16

The posters need to be really snazzy, just like my flashy polka-dot sweater that I wear on special occasions.

I got out every glitter pen, magic marker, paint bottle, and sticker sheet I could find, and Maty and I went wild!

17

Mom said to just make sure and be back before
dinner. I grabbed my bike, Maty hopped in her dog
wagon, and we were off!

F.Y.I.
Maty is sitting
on
the
posters.

We stapled, glued, and taped posters all over town.

When we got to Dad's bike shop, he gave me a big hug and Maty a dog biscuit and said to go ahead and put a poster in the front window.

We got a little carried away and sort of wallpapered the WHOLE window.

It looks really great.

Since we used up all the posters, we decided we'd better head home. We were almost out the door when all of a sudden Maty started to bark and bark and bark. Really loud.

Maty raced over to some kids who were taking down our posters, crumpling them up, and throwing them in the trash!

I suddenly realized that these were NOT ordinary kids . . .

Snobby →

← Annoying

They were the one and only ICKY VICKY and her
mean little brother Dicky.

Maty started to run circles around them, making Vicky and Dicky stop dead in their tracks. (Boy, do I have the greatest dog in the whole wide world or what?)

Icky Vicky and Dicky looked super scared. I even felt a teeny tiny bit sorry for them, so I asked Maty to sit (which she does perfectly, by the way).

I looked them both straight in the eye and told them to get their grubby little hands off of our posters! Icky Vicky just started to laugh. And laugh. And laugh.

She pointed at Maty and said, "How could a three-legged mutt and a kooky girl like you ever think you'd be able to rescue anything?!"

Icky Vicky went on and on about how she and Dicky had gotten to level 800 million (or something like that) on the newest animal rescue video game that their dad just bought them.

She thinks they're "expert" animal rescuers now. "SO WHAT!" I yelled back. "All you two do is stare at a stupid screen and save totally FAKE animals from totally FAKE bad guys."

I continued: "Because if you hadn't noticed, video game animals aren't real! Who cares about how many cartoon animals you help. I sure don't." See, Maty and I are the . . .

. . . and I told Icky Vicky that if she said anything else mean about Maty, well . . .

Just then my dad walked up. He'd heard all the commotion and said Maty and I needed to get going. He had just gotten off the phone with Mom and she was waiting for us at home.

I looked at Vicky and Dicky and told them in my sweetest "I can't stand you" voice to please leave our posters alone. And to make sure to NEVER call us if they ever needed any help finding any of their pets.

I could tell that Dad wasn't too happy, so I knew we better leave pronto. I gave him a quick hug, called Maty, and we were on our way.

We needed to get home. It was getting late, and now that our posters are everywhere, we could be called into action at any moment!

## CHAPTER TWO

Maty and I woke up bright and early. I was so excited to be an official animal rescuer that I couldn't stay in bed a minute longer.

Mom called us down for breakfast. I was right in the middle of eating my huge stack of waffles with whipped cream and strawberries when the phone rang.

It was George. I asked him if I could call him right back because my whipped cream was melting, but he said it couldn't wait.

He'd just been at Dizzy Donuts having a huge delicious donut with his dad and sister like they do every weekend.

He saw our poster and thought it was really cool. When he went back home, he stopped at his friend Otto's apartment to feed Otto's pet rat. His name is Roger.

Otto and his family are in Disneyland, and George is rodent sitting. (Rodent is a fancy word for rat.)

Anyway, when he got to Otto's apartment, the cage was empty!

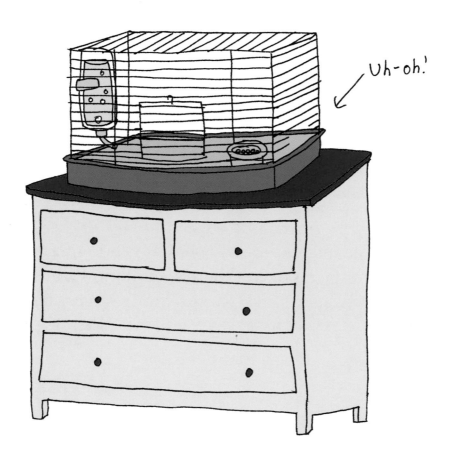

Uh-oh!

34

No Roger the rat. Gonzo. Disappeared. Roger had
run away.

George didn't know what to do . . . and then his sister
reminded him about my poster. So that's why he's calling
and that's why my waffles are now soggy and gross.
   George wants to know if there's anything I can do
to help him find Roger before Otto gets back home
tomorrow . . . or else George is afraid that Otto might go
berserk!

Because Otto really, really loves his rat.

And I guess Roger isn't just any old rat. He's a Dumbo
rat. A super smart Dumbo rat.

I asked George to hold on a minute. I needed to start
writing some stuff down . . .

Date: <u>Saturday</u>
NOTES TO ME:
* Our first rescue! We need to do a great job.

(But YIKES! I know nothing about rats, let alone Dumbo rats. Isn't Dumbo a flying elephant?)

*Did George really say that Otto gets back TOMORROW? That means we have ONE day to find him! <u>DOUBLE YIKES!!!</u>

I played it cool and told George not to worry. Of course we'll help him find Otto's rat. Maty and I just need to brush up on a few rat facts, but then we'll be over in a jiffy.

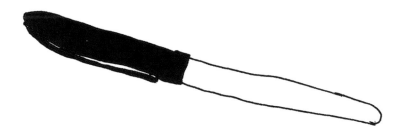

Mom put some fresh waffles on my plate, and I topped them off with tons of whipped cream. Then I loaded up Maty's kibble bowl.

We need our strength. We're going to be very busy girls.

I sat down and started to take some more notes:

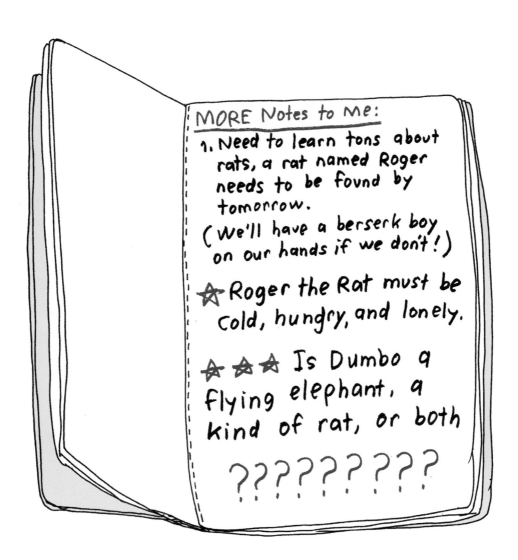

If I'm going to rescue a rat, I need to think like a rat.

I got on the computer and started to read everything I could about the smart little rodents.

And then I wrote all the important stuff down in my notebook . . .

# RAT FACTS:

1. Dumbo is a flying circus elephant AND a kind of rat (a really cute rat with big ears!).
2. Rats are very smart, the smartest of all the rodents.
3. Rats laugh with a high chirping sound when they think something is funny.
4. They have belly buttons.
5. A rat's fur smells like grape soda.
6. Rats are very curious!
7. Their teeth are never stop growing and are very, very sharp. They can even chew through cement + metal.

8. Rats have been sent into space!

9. Of all rodents, rats are most like dogs. They can be trained to come, sit, beg, fetch, and jump through a hoop! ← (Sounds like Matty.)

10. Just like dogs, rats really love their owners and miss them when they're away.

11. Rats can use a litterbox!

12. Rats are expert swimmers. They can swim for a long time without a break and can keep themselves floating for three days.

13. They really love chocolate. ♥ ♥ ♥ 🍫 ♥ *YUM*.

Maty was ready for a break. I let her out in the backyard and went to find Mom to tell her that we're headed out.

Then I called George and said we'd meet him at Otto's apartment.

I'm feeling better about things, now that I understand rats. They're actually super cool animals.

Who knows, there might even be a Dumbo rat in my future (a girl can dream, can't she?). But first things first . . . let's find Roger.

CHAPTER THREE

Maty and I parked our bike and wagon outside Otto's apartment building. We ran up the stairs to the second floor and knocked on 2B.

George answered and said he was sure glad to see us. Staring at Roger's empty cage was making him really sad.

We walked back to Otto's bedroom and there on his chest of drawers was a metal cage with a small hole in the side.

THE HOLE!!!

Roger had chewed through the wire . . . that's how he escaped.

# ☆Rat Fact #7:

Rat teeth are very, very sharp and can even chew through METAL!

Maty got right to work. She sniffed under Otto's bed, in his closet, and under his desk. Nothing. Nada. No Roger.

I decided I better ask George some questions and look around the room for clues.

I took out my notebook and started to write stuff down:

☆ Day: Saturday 🤍🤍🤍

Clues:

-George said that Roger was acting weird last night. He didn't eat his dinner and was running around crazy-like in his cage.

-This is the first time George has taken care of Roger. Otto has never left Roger alone because he thought he would be too lonely.

✳ (Rat Fact #10: Rats are like dogs and really miss their owners when they're gone...)

Hmmm, maybe that's it . . . maybe Roger missed Otto SO much that he chewed through his cage so he could go find him!

He could never make it all the way to Disneyland.

But where would Roger go to look for Otto?

And then I noticed something across the room . . . a
bulletin board full of photos.

It looks like Otto and
Roger go everywhere
together. Roger rides on
Otto's shoulder or in his
coat pocket.

There's a picture of them at the library:

At the swimming pool:

At his grandma's house:

And what's this?

A first-place ribbon from Pom-Pom Pie Place? I guess Otto and Roger won the pie eating contest last month.

And from the looks of the picture, they ate a ton of chocolate cream pie.

## ☆ Rat Fact #13: Rats LOVE Chocolate!

I looked at George and said I think I might know where Roger went . . .

Roger loves chocolate, he's looking for Otto, and rats can smell yummy stuff from miles away.

Pom-Pom Pie Place, here we come!

## CHAPTER FOUR

Maty, George, and I cruised down to Pom-Pom Pie Place and burst through the door.

The nice lady at the counter asked if she could help us and told us about the special of the day: Blueberry Very Berry Pie. She said it has TONS of blueberries in it.

We told her we're looking for a rat named Roger. He comes in a lot with his owner, Otto. Actually, they won the pie eating contest a little while ago.

We're just wondering if Roger's been in for pie lately? Has she seen him crawling around?

She said of course she knows Roger—he's the cutest Dumbo rat she's ever met. But he and Otto haven't been in to the pie shop for over a week.

I asked if we could look around a little. She said to go right ahead and to let her know if we needed any help.

I also decided to get a piece of Blueberry Very Berry Pie to go (it's my favorite).

Maty started right in—she sniffed under the tables.

George looked in the bathroom.

And I decided to walk around the outside of the building. I'm not sure what I was looking for, but I just had a feeling.

Sure enough, outside the back door was a trail of pie crumbs and a whole bunch of tiny blue footprints.

Yep, Roger had been here all right and had helped himself to a piece of the special of the day: Blueberry Very Berry Pie.

I ran back inside and got Maty and George (and my piece of pie) and told them what I'd found.

We rushed outside. George screamed, he was so excited. We were on the right track, but still no Roger. I took out my notebook and wrote down the latest clues:

Day: Still Saturday

Clues:

1. The first Roger sighting is at Pom-Pom Pie Place!
2. There's a trail of pie crumbs out the back door...
3. There are tiny blue rat footprints—his feet must have been covered with berries!
4. Because the pie of the day is BLUEBERRY VERY BERRY.
   ★ Yes, it's my favorite and I did get a piece to go
5. George is very excited that we have spotted Roger.
6. The day is zooming by, We need to find Roger fast.

George decided to follow the footprints. They got lighter and lighter and then just faded away. All the berry juice must have worn off Roger's little paws. The trail just ended.

Suddenly George was sad again. I told George to keep his chin up. I just know we'll find Roger.

And then out of the blue, Maty started to bark and took off running. George and I grabbed our bikes and followed her.

This wasn't like Maty, but I had a feeling she knew exactly what she was doing. My guess is that she knows where Roger is. Boy . . . do I have a great rescue dog or what?

CHAPTER FIVE

Maty was running full speed ahead. As she rounded
the corner, I finally figured out what was going on.

There was a super high-pitched sound coming from
up ahead.

A girl was screaming at the top of her lungs. And it
wasn't just any old scream—it was a screeching sound
that only one girl in the whole wide world could make.

It was Icky Vicky.

Maty had heard the sound all the way back at the pie shop.

Sure enough, Maty led us to the swimming pool, where Icky Vicky was screaming her head off and tons of kids were all standing around the pool.

George and I broke through the crowd and couldn't believe our eyes!

3FT

And then I remembered . . .

one of the pictures of Otto and Roger was at the pool.

Roger had come here after the pie shop to find Otto!

As soon as the kids saw a rat in the pool, they'd freaked out and got out pronto.

Everyone, that is, except one little boy who had his mask and snorkel on and didn't know Roger was in the pool.

And that little snorkel boy was the one and only Dicky.
That's why Icky Vicky had been screaming her head off.

George and I gave each other a huge high five, and I
gave Maty a high paw.

We did it. We found Roger! And we scared the pants off Icky Vicky. (Wow, what a bonus.)

Finally Dicky saw Roger and started to go totally nuts. I told him if he did anything to Roger he'd pay for it big time. I ran and got my piece of pie out of Maty's wagon.

### Rat Fact #9:

Of all rodents, rats are most like dogs. They can be trained to come when called!

We asked all the kids around the pool to be quiet, and George knelt down and called Roger's name. Then he held out the piece of pie.

3FT

Sure enough, Roger swam over to George and jumped right onto his shoulder!

George fed him bits of berry pie and had a smile on his face a mile wide.

We did it! Operation Rat Rescue was complete

All the kids started to clap—except Vicky and Dicky, of course. They just ran off yelling and screaming at each other.

George, Maty, Roger, and I all headed back to Otto's apartment. Roger the rat was no longer on the loose. was safe and sound in Maty's dog wagon eating the rest of my Blueberry Very Berry Pie.

I have to say, it's sure been a VERY berry good day.

## CHAPTER SIX

When we got back to Otto's apartment, we remembered that Roger's cage had a huge hole in it.

We called George's mom and asked if she could bring over George's old guinea pig cage. It was in his closet. She dropped it off, and we put all of Roger's stuff in it to make him feel at home.

I told George that he should probably take Roger and the cage back to his apartment. That way he could keep him company until Otto got home.

I picked Roger up and gave him a little kiss on the nose.

I said I was glad there was a happy ending and to stay put because Otto would be back before he knew it.

Maty and I said goodbye to George. I was starving and knew my mom would be wondering where we were.

George thanked us a ton and said he'd tell everyone he knows about how we rescued Roger. He thinks Maty and I are the most awesome animal rescuers ever!

I have to say, so do I.

## CHAPTER SEVEN

When we got home,
Mom had my favorite
peanut butter and
banana sandwich ready
and two peanut butter
treats for Maty.

I told her all about our
adventure. She gave me
a huge hug and said she
was so proud of us.

And she was also super glad that a scared, lost little
rat was now home safe and sound because of us.

I took out my notebook and decided I better finish it
up. My first rescue notebook needed a happy ending.

**Day: Yes, it's still Saturday**

★ Happy ending and stuff! ★

❀ We found Roger the Rat in a swimming pool. He's a very good swimmer.

✿ He's now safe at home in George's old guinea pig cage because his had a hole in it. (Roger chewed through his cage with his sharp teeth to escape!)

❀ Roger is staying with George tonight so he doesn't get lonely.

-Otto will be so happy to see Roger when he gets home from Disneyland! 😊😊😊

-Maty is a hero! She found Roger.

＊Maybe Maty is super-duper good at rescuing animals because I rescued her from the shelter???

I CAN'T WAIT to help another furry friend, because it really makes me feel happy inside... even better than a big piece of pie.

I decided I better call Aunt Bee and thank her for the notebook and bandana and tell her all about my day. And ask her to send MORE notebooks, because after today, I have a feeling we'll be needing them!

Lost or hurt animals, have no fear . . . Mimi and Maty are here!

The sign reads: Meet the REAL Mimi and Maty

Mimi has always loved animals. When she was seven years old, she started a rescue notebook so she could keep track of all the animals she's helped: butterflies, birds, chipmunks . . . even a rainbow trout!

When Mimi was eleven years old, she wanted to help feed the dogs and cats at her local shelter in Bend, Oregon, so she created the website Freekibble.com. Freekibble has now fed over eight million meals to homeless pets at shelters and rescues all over the country.

Maty is now the Humane Society of Central Oregon's goodwill ambassador. She visits schools and groups, teaching people about animal safety and showcasing the many abilities of a disabled dog. Maty is also the first three-legged dog to qualify and compete in two Skyhoundz World Canine Disc Dog Championships. Way to go, Maty!

Mimi and Maty met through their work at the animal shelter and have been special friends ever since. With their big hearts, Mimi and Maty continue to inspire others to help care for and love animals.

## About the Author

Brooke Smith is Mimi's mom. She has always wanted to write a book inspired by Mimi's big heart and all the fun she has helping animals. With this book, Brooke hopes to get other kids excited to help all of the four- and three-legged creatures that need them.

## About the Illustrator

Alli Arnold is never without a pen and paper. Her first illustration was published when she was just seven years old, and she has gone on to illustrate for such clients as the *New York Times* and Bergdorf Goodman. Alli lives in New York City with her little dog, Nino. To see more of Alli's drawings, go to www.alliarnold.com.